For my Grandchildren

The Robin That Couldn't Sing

Illustrated by Carol Patten

written by Andy Mitchell

Robin was hatched
in a nest in the
front of an old car
parked in the
corner of an
orchard.

Early in April all
the birds around were
singing when Robin
left the nest.

Soon Robin was flying
and spent each day
high up in a larch
tree.

Having spent all his early life
with his parents, he was now more interested
in things in his bright new world.

At first Robin thought that he could go anywhere but robins are very aggressive, and when he went too near another robin family`s nest, he was made most unwelcome.

"What do you think you are doing in our territory?" shouted another robin who then dived at him and turned away at the last moment.

"Sorry, I didn`t know you felt that way, I won`t do it again."

Up in the highest
branches in a larch he
was not bothered by the
two families of other
birds nesting there.

A pair of goldcrests and a
pair of blue tits.

They chatted away
about all kinds of bird
things.

But one morning Robin
noticed a change. Until
that day everything stayed
the same but now there was
a strong breeze and the top
branches were moving wildly.

"Suddenly Robin heard a strange voice."

"Hi there little bird, I dare you to fly while I am blowing like this."

He had trouble understanding the strange way that the wind spoke but when he did, he replied.

"I would be mad to try while you are blowing like this."

"Be brave, come up here where I can see you properly and I can take you miles away."

"How do I know where I will end up? You might take me somewhere that robins don`t want to live, far away."

"You will get bored messing about in the same place all your life."

"Alright Mister Wind, because robins have to spread out when we are a few months old, I will come with you and see a bit of the world."

And with that he flew up where the wind was blowing hardest.

Robin was surprised to find that he was taken along with no effort at all.

"Where are we going to?"

"Just settle down and don`t ask so many questions. Then you will learn more," said the Wind in a grumpy voice.

Soon Robin began to worry about resting for the night.

"I know, I know," said the Wind.

"You want something to eat before you rest,
but what you don`t know is that I rest too. You will learn that
there are times of day after a storm when things get quiet, and this is one
of them now." With that the wind slowed and Robin flew down to a farmyard.

Robin easily found plenty of food, then he met some sparrows and asked them about the place.

"But how did you get here?" one sparrow asked.

"We saw you coming down from away up high and thought it a bit strange."

"The Wind dared me to fly up to him and go travelling."

"I`ve never heard of that."

"We don`t go travelling and are happy here as the farmer leaves things alone and we can get on with life without flying with the Wind."

Robin didn`t think much of this, as he wasn`t a sparrow and it was getting dark, he flew up to a high branch nearby and tucking his head under his wing went to sleep.

Just before dawn the chorus of birdsong woke him.

It made Robin feel sad as he was now on his own. Just at that moment the Wind came along.

"Are you ready," he called to Robin.

"I certainly am," replied Robin, "Where to today?"

tweet!

tweet!

"Just stop asking questions then you will learn more.

Yesterday was just to see if you could be brave. Today you will see some wonderful things."

"Can I ask you one more question?"

"Yes, so long as it is a sensible one."

"When we wake up, robins are nearly always the first birds to sing and the first thing I heard today was another robin, I have tried to sing but nothing happens. Do you think I will ever be able to sing?"

"Things don`t happen all at once.

How old are you?"

"Only two months and four days," replied Robin counting the days.

"Well, I`m not sure but I think that robins don`t sing until they have beautiful red breasts."

"Well, I certainly don`t have that yet."

"So what are you worrying about then."

While they had been talking they travelled over the south coast of England.

Down below Robin could see some islands and soon after that the coast of another country.

"Now you will spend tonight in France, and you will find things different there."

"What do you mean?"

"You may find other birds that look a bit like robins but aren`t."

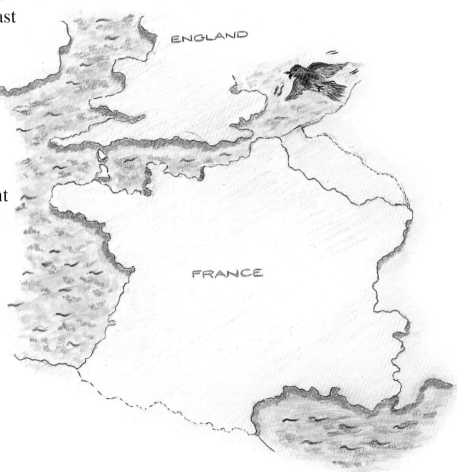

Sure enough he found that the nightingales take the place of robins in gardens and parks in France.

They are close relations but a robin has a red breast and nightingales don`t.

Robin was not prepared for what happened later. Just when he was going to sleep, there was an almighty trill and the nightingale had begun his song.

"We robins have the sense to sing in the daytime," he shouted , but the nightingale just went on and on.

Robin had to do his best to ignore all this night time entertainment.

The next day the Wind stopped blowing to give everyone a rest. They had arrived at a huge lake in the Pyrenees Mountains.

The swallows were gathering there on their way back to Africa.

There were so many that there was hardly anywhere for Robin to perch.

"Where are you all going," he asked one of the swallows.

"To Africa of course, we don`t like cold winters and spend ours over there.

It takes about a month, we stop here for a rest in spring on our way north, so we stop here again on our way back, we have always done it that way."

So the Wind found Robin a few weeks later.

"Are you ready to go home or do you want to stay here?"

"I had better go back home. There are lots of reasons but most of all, I miss other robins."

"I will blow north in a couple of weeks, so I will take you back then," said the Wind with a big sigh.

"Thanks, that will be great."

In the next two weeks while he was waiting for the Wind to return Robin met several strange looking birds. "Who are you?"

"I am a Hoopoe," cried the colourful bird and raised and folded his handsome crest.

" I am a Bluethroat," said the small bright bird.

Several days after that he saw three birds that he recognised, they were robins but they came from Eastern Europe.

That evening they all sang together but he was still only making a chirping sound.

"This is really embarrassing," he said.

One of them said that when he was young he had heard that in summer. But he also said that a robin`s song changes to a lovely winter tune in the autumn.

"Not much chance of me being able to do that," said Robin.

"That will come," said one of the Easterners, I was nearly a year old before I could sing.

"Even then it was not what I can do now."   With that he trilled away merrily.

Soon the Wind returned and Robin suggested that the other robins came back with him to England. He decided to keep his reason to himself. They all agreed but only after the Wind promised to take them home again.

Then the Wind later picked a quiet moment when he and Robin were alone.

"You like that lady robin, don`t you?"

"How did you work that out?"

"Oh I can see these things."

"But how can I persuade her to stay with me in England?"

"Well I think you will have to learn to sing."

"But you know how hard I have tried already."

"Yes, yes," said the wind, come up high with me then close your wings almost completely. While you are diving down faster and faster, listen carefully and you will hear all the angels singing in heaven. You will want to sing too, your song will come out in great bursts of joy. But still there was nothing coming from Robin himself. As he arrived back near the ground he saw the girl robin and felt a great swell of pride. He noticed the way she was looking back at him.

At first only a little trill came but he was so pleased that anything had happened at all, he tried again.

Very suddenly the little wispy trill became louder and louder until the Wind shouted down, "Stop all that racket, I told you how you might learn and now I am telling you to stop, you should use your voice sparingly."

And this is what Robin has been doing ever since.

And no, I haven`t forgotten to tell you what happened next. But you probably guessed.

After they arrived back in England, the other two got bored with the way Robin and his girl friend were always together. So the next time the Wind came by they took a ride back to Eastern Europe.

Then Robin built his first nest and soon after that there were four beautiful blue eggs in it. Every morning Robin`s was the first song to be heard and every evening the last.

Fourteen days later four baby robins hatched and soon they were ready to leave the nest.

That is the end of this story but not really because of all the baby robins and everything that happened to them too.